Who Needs Glasses?

by Fran Manushkin

illustrated by Tammie Lyon

raintree

a Capstone company — publishers for children

Raintree is an imprint of Capstone Global Library Limited, a company incorporated in England and Wales having its registered office at 264 Banbury Road, Oxford, OX2 7DY – Registered company number: 6695582

www.raintree.co.uk
myorders@raintree.co.uk

Art Director: Kay Fraser
Graphic Designer: Kristi Carlson
Printed and bound in India

ISBN 978 1 4747 8223 4
23 22 21 20 19
10 9 8 7 6 5 4 3 2 1

British Library Cataloguing in Publication Data
A full catalogue record for this book is available from the British Library.

Acknowledgements
Greg Holch, pg. 26
Tammie Lyon, pg. 26

Contents

Chapter 1

Dinosaurs

"Today's lesson is about dinosaurs," said Miss Winkle. "This dinosaur is called Sue. It was named after the lady who found the bones."

"Cool!" said Katie.

Miss Winkle asked Pedro to read to the class. “I can’t,” he said. “My book is blurry.”

“It’s not,” said Miss Winkle. “I think you need to get your eyes tested.”

A few days later, Pedro showed Katie his new glasses.

"I feel a bit weird," said Pedro.

"You look great!" said Katie.

“Today,” said Miss Winkle, “we are making a dinosaur scene. You will work in teams of three.”

Chapter 2
Glasses gone missing

"Let's be a team," Katie told Pedro and JoJo. They began to work.

"Where are your glasses?" Katie asked Pedro.

"Um . . . I think I've lost them," Pedro said.

Pedro began to read from his book. “Most dinosaurs ate pants.”

“No!” said Katie, laughing. “Not pants – plants!”

“Oh! Right!” said Pedro.

Pedro read another dinosaur fact: "The word 'dinosaur' means terrible blizzard."

"No!" Katie told him. "It's terrible lizard!"

"I'd better read the facts," Katie told Pedro. "You can start making our scene."

"Great!" Pedro said. "I love drawing!"

Pedro drew a dinosaur.

"That looks like my cat," said Barry, the new boy.

Pedro squinted at his drawing. Katie said, "I wish you could find your glasses."

During break, Katie had an idea. She came back to class without her glasses.

"Where are they?" asked Pedro.

"I don't know," said Katie. "But I don't really need them."

Katie sat down.

"Watch out!" warned JoJo. "You are sitting on the clay for our scene."

"Oops!" said Katie. "I didn't see that."

"I can make a paper dinosaur," said Katie. She squinted as she folded the paper.

"That looks like a boat," said Barry. "Your team is very funny!"

"I don't think so," sighed JoJo.

Chapter 3
Project saved!

"Our project is a mess!" said Katie. "And we are running out of time. If only I could find my glasses, then I could see!"

“Look!” said Pedro suddenly. “I’ve found mine! They were in my pocket the whole time!”

Pedro began to work. He made a terrific clay dinosaur, and he painted a scary volcano.

"Looking good!" cheered Katie and JoJo.

"Very good!" agreed Barry.

"Hey!" said Katie. "Guess what? I've found my glasses too. They were in my pocket the whole time!"

Pedro laughed. “Katie,

you are very tricky!”

“Maybe,” said Katie.

She laughed too.

JoJo told Pedro, "You look clever in your glasses."

"I feel clever," he said, admiring his work.

Miss Winkle admired it too.

She took photos of all the teams and their projects.

Katie and Pedro and JoJo smiled proudly.

"You look terrific!" Miss Winkle said.

And they did!

About the author

Fran Manushkin is the author of many popular picture books, including *Baby, Come Out!*; *Latkes and Applesauce: A Hanukkah Story*; *The Belly Book* and *Big Girl Panties*. There is a real Katie Woo - she's Fran'sgreat-niece - but she never gets in half the trouble that Katie Woo does in the books. Fran writes on her beloved Mac computer in New York City, USA, without the help of her two naughty cats, Chaim and Goldy.

About the illustrator

Tammie Lyon began her love for drawing at a young age while sitting at the kitchen table with her dad. She continued her love of art and eventually attended college, where she earned a bachelors degree in fine art. After a brief career as a professional ballet dancer, she decided to devote herself full time to illustration. Today she lives with her husband, Lee, in Cincinnati, Ohio, USA. Her dogs, Gus and Dudley, keep her company as she works in her studio.

Glossary

admiring looking at something and enjoying it

blizzard a heavy snowstorm

blurry fuzzy and unclear

projects school tasks that are worked on over a period of time

scene model made by placing figures and other objects in front of a painted background

squinted nearly closed eyes in order to see more clearly

terrific very good or excellent

volcano a mountain with vents through which molten lava, ash, cinders and gas erupt

Discussion questions

1. Have you ever worked on a project with partners? Did you like it? Why or why not?

2. Why do you think Pedro did not want to wear his glasses?

3. Why are glasses important? What examples in the story explain why glasses are important?

Writing prompts

1. Pretend you are choosing some glasses. Write a paragraph to describe what the perfect pair of glasses look like. What colour are they? What about shape?

2. Make a sign that talks about how great glasses are. Make sure you include a picture.

3. Katie's class was learning about dinosaurs. List three facts about dinosaurs. If you can't think of three, ask a grown-up to help you find some in a book or on the computer.

Having fun with Katie Woo!

Glamour glasses

Katie Woo loves her blue glasses. They are stylish, and best of all, they help her see. You can make your own glasses using pipe cleaners. They won't change how you see, but they will give you a new look for some fashion fun!

What you need:

- 4 pipe cleaners
- ruler
- scissors
- a variety of small jewels, pom poms or other decorations
- glue

What you do:

1. Using the ruler to measure, cut two pipe cleaners so they are 20 centimetres long.

2. Take one of the 20-cm pipe cleaners and form it into the shape of your choice. You could make a circle, heart or square. Repeat with the other 20-cm pipe cleaner. These are the "lenses".

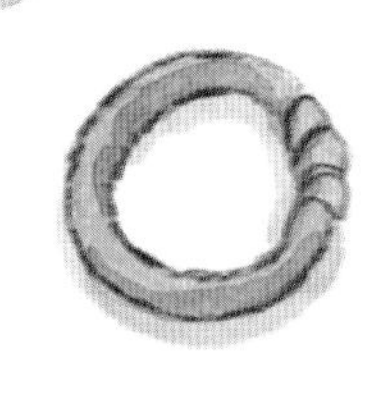

3. Take a third pipe cleaner and fold it in half. Twist the two halves together.
4. Use the twisted pipe cleaner to connect your "lenses". For best results, wrap each end around the lenses 3-4 times.
5. Cut the last pipe cleaner in half. Twist each piece around the lense section to make the legs of the frame. Add a curve at the ends so the glasses fit around your ears.
6. Now you can decorate your glasses! Attach jewels, poms poms or other small decorations with glue. Leave to dry.

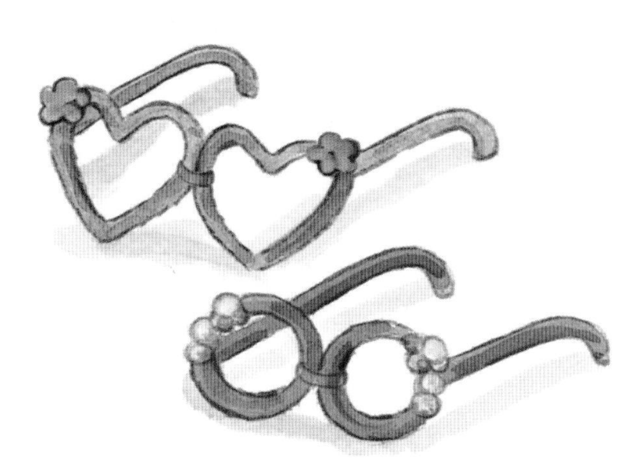